TJ and the Cats

AN
ORCA
YOUNG
READER

TJ
and the
Cats

Hazel Hutchins

ORCA BOOK PUBLISHERS

National Library of Canada Cataloguing in Publication Data
Hutchins, H.J. (Hazel J.)

TJ and the cats

ISBN 1-55143-205-6

I. Title. PS8565.U826T62 2002 jC813'.54 C2001-911750-7

PZ7.H96163Tj 2002

Library of Congress Catalog Card Number: 2001099445

Orca Book Publishers gratefully acknowledges the support of
our publishing programs provided by the following agencies:
the Department of Canadian Heritage, The Canada Council
for the Arts, and the British Columbia Arts Council.

Cover design by Christine Toller
Cover & interior illustrations by Krysten Brooker

Printed and bound in Canada

IN CANADA
Orca Book Publishers
PO Box 5626, Station B
Victoria, BC Canada
V8R 6S4

IN THE UNITED STATES
Orca Book Publishers
PO Box 468
Custer, WA USA
98240-0468

04 03 02 • 5 4 3 2 1

Special thanks to Dr. Sylvia McAllister, DVM, for providing story consultation in addition to expert pet care on so many occasions; my brother Lawrence for starting the whole thing with the "fact" that cats gain weight as they sleep across one's feet at night; and my husband Ted, who has always felt that life is just that much better with a cat (or two) in the house.

H.H.

Chapter 1

My name is TJ Barnes and I don't like cats.

I don't like the way they stare. I don't like the way they slink. I don't like the way they race under your feet, slash without warning and wash their behinds in public. Cats give me the creeps.

If I'd remembered all these details when my grandmother phoned, it would have saved me a whole lot of trouble.

"TJ," said Gran, "I've got a problem."

It was early Monday morning. Gran wasn't supposed to be on the phone.

She was supposed to be on a plane to Hawaii.

"What happened?" I asked her. "Was there a tidal wave? An earthquake? Did the plane get hijacked?"

Gran had been looking forward to her trip to Hawaii forever.

"Worse," said Gran. "I'm about to leave for the airport and my cat sitter has canceled. Can you fill in?"

"Sure," I said, the words just flying out before I could stop them. "Sure, I can help."

"Thanks, TJ," said Gran. "I'll send them right over by taxi."

An awful feeling slid along the little hairs on the back of my neck and trickled down the top of my spine.

"Here?" I asked. "You're sending them over here?"

"My house is too far for you to come every day," said Gran. "Keep them in your laundry room until they get used to the place. Thank you, *thank you,* TJ. Aloha."

"Aloha," I said, but Gran had already hung up.

I stared at the phone. What had I done? I thought I was agreeing to go over to Gran's house to drop a few kibbles in a cat dish. I didn't want all four cats to come and live at our place!

I picked up the phone and dialed Mom and Dad at the store. The line was busy. It was always busy these days. I hung up. I walked around in a circle.

My Gran was the world's greatest grandmother. She could build models, fly kites, devise secret codes and open locks without a combination. She deserved to go to Hawaii.

I'd almost convinced myself that things were going to be okay when the taxi arrived. I went out to meet it. The driver was a mess. His eyes were wild. His shoulders were covered in cat hair. There were scratches all over his arms.

"Watch out for little old ladies asking favors," he said. "And take this one into the house right away. It knows how to escape."

He handed me a carry-box painted with jungle vines. Out of a hole at the

side curled a long, sharp claw and a tuft of black fur. The funny little chill trickled down my spine again. I remembered the name of Gran's black cat. Killer.

I carried the box into the house and set it in the laundry room. I went back outside. The taxi driver was setting three more boxes and all sorts of cat gear on the sidewalk.

Yeowl. Meeowl. Hiss, said the boxes.

The driver shuddered with each howl.

"She really is the world's greatest grandmother," I said.

"She owns the world's most miserable cats," said the taxi driver. "Aloha."

He jumped back in the cab and drove off. I stayed on the sidewalk with three howling cat boxes.

The first box was painted with swirls of color and silver stars. The name *Cleo* was painted over the door. Cleo had long fluffy hair all gray and white and salmon-colored. Gran thought she was the most beautiful cat in the world.

The second box was painted like the fun house at the fair. *Kink* said the name. He was the orange one with a bent tail. Gran called him a clown.

The last box was twice the size of the other two and had fancy gold paint. That had to be Maximilian the Emperor — Max for short.

Yeowl. Meeowl. Hiss.

I began to leapfrog the boxes and gear up the sidewalk to the house. Cleo and Kink howled all the way. Max got heavier. I'm sure he got heavier.

Just as I was nearing our side door, the neighbors' dog got wind of what was happening. He rushed the house.

Cats! he barked. *Catscatscatscats!*

I tossed the boxes into the entrance, leapt in after them and banged the door shut behind me. *Thump, thump, thump, thump, thump.* It took me a full minute to figure out the thumping was my own heart, panic-beating in my chest.

I took the boxes and the cat gear to the laundry room. I set food and water at one side of the room. I set clean kitty litter at the other side of the room. I tried not to think about dirty kitty litter. One by one I opened the boxes and looked in.

Cleo's green eyes peered out of the first box.

Kink's yellow eyes peered out of the second box.

Max's blue eyes peered out of the third box — actually Max's eyes didn't peer, they blazed brilliantly from a heap of white fur. The emperor was furious.

I reached down to open the last box. It was already open. That funny little feeling was sliding down my spine again. Killer had set herself free.

She wasn't in the laundry room. She wasn't in the hall. I didn't find her in the rest of the house. I wasn't sure I wanted to. I put an extra tray of kitty litter and some food in the hallway. I was feeling stranger and stranger about having cats in the house. Cats give me the creeps.

I phoned my friend Seymour.

"Hurrah!" he said. "The school burnt down!"

That's what he always says if I phone him before school.

"No such luck," I said. "I have to

ask you something. Do you like cats?"

"What's there to like?" asked Seymour.

"Exactly," I said.

"Is that all?" asked Seymour. "You don't have any news about the school mysteriously dropping off the face of the earth?"

"That's all," I said.

"Rats," said Seymour.

For the second time that morning someone hung up before I had time to say goodbye.

As I left for school I remembered a story about a sailor who couldn't swim but didn't tell anyone. He fell overboard and no one tried to rescue him. He drowned.

That was the way it was with me and cats. Gran didn't know they gave me the creeps, and I'd been too slow to tell her. Now I was about to drown.

I had to find some way to keep my head above water. I had to learn to float or dog paddle or grab onto a passing log.

Sometimes just being alive drives me crazy.

Chapter 2

Our teacher, Ms. Kovalski, is a witch.

She's not a horrible witch, just the sort of witch that knows things. I was sitting in science class staring at an open book, but she knew I wasn't really reading. Teachers like that shouldn't be allowed.

"That's enough daydreaming, TJ," she said.

I wasn't daydreaming. I was being haunted. Every time I looked at the page, all I saw were one pair of green eyes, one pair of yellow eyes, one pair of furious blue eyes and Killer's long, curved claw. It had been like that all morning. If I didn't do something soon

I really was going to drown.

"What subject have you and Seymour chosen for your report?" asked Ms. K.

"Cats," I said.

It just slipped out, but right away it looked like a rescue log floating by.

Seymour began waving his arms around. He almost hit Amanda Baker in the head by accident, except she's good at ducking. Actually, Amanda's good at everything.

"No we're not!" said Seymour. "We're doing dinosaurs!"

"I changed it," I said.

"You can't change it!" said Seymour.

"Yes I can," I said. "You chose for the last report. This time it's my turn."

"You already chose," said Seymour. "You agreed on dinosaurs!"

Seymour has done dinosaur reports three years in a row. He should have been glad to change.

"Excuse me, Seymour," said Ms. K. She is very polite for a witch. "TJ, if you're doing a report on cats, why are you pretending to read a book about dinosaurs?"

"That's why I'm only *pretending* to read," I said. "May Seymour and I go to the library and get books on cats?"

Ms. K. looked at Seymour. He was scowling — hard.

"That would be an excellent idea," she said. "Please work things out on the way."

Seymour is not very good at working things out.

"I don't want to do a report on cats!" he said in the hall.

"Know your enemy," I said.

"They aren't my enemies," said Seymour. "We just don't get along. I told you that on the phone. What's there to like about cats?"

"Exactly," I said.

"What do you mean, 'exactly'?" said Seymour.

"People always do reports on things they like," I said. "We should be different. We should do a report on something we don't like."

I was feeling too strange about the cats to tell Seymour about them outright.

"Weird," said Seymour.

It was just weird enough for him to be interested. Seymour's that kind of kid. Besides, we managed to use up the entire period in the library. That's a lot more fun than sitting in class.

"Do you want to get together after school and try the cat report? When it doesn't work, we can go back to dinosaurs," said Seymour as we carried the cat books to class.

"Not tonight," I said. "I have to clean my room tonight."

Seymour stopped, looked at me in horror and fell down in a dead faint in the middle of the hall.

"Seymour!"

He just lay there.

"The principal's coming!" I said.

"No she's not," said Seymour, but he jumped to his feet anyway. "Wait, I get it! It must be opposite week. We do reports on subjects we don't like. We clean our room. We eat broccoli. We refuse to watch TV. We could drive all sorts of adults crazy this way."

"Sure," I said. "It's a great idea."

"Count me out," said Seymour.

"Seymour!" I said.

"All right, I'll do the cat report with you," said Seymour, "but forget about the rest of it. All the adults I know are crazy enough already."

Chapter 3

Every once in a while Seymour is right on the mark. His statement about adults being crazy described what it was like at our house these days.

"The store was busier than ever today," said Mom as she came flying into the house with groceries.

"You should have seen the size of the paint order that came in, TJ," said Dad as he began to organize supper. "Even then they forgot half of it."

"I forgot to phone the suppliers," said Mom. "I'd better leave a message on their answering machine."

"I've got to call Pete's Painting tomorrow," said Dad.

Mom picked up the phone and began to dial. Dad took out his pocket recorder and began to leave messages to himself while he cooked. It was as if they'd suddenly vanished from the kitchen. Their bodies were there but their brains had been stolen by hardware aliens. I went down to the laundry room.

The cats were still in their boxes. As far as I could tell they'd been in their boxes since morning. Whether I liked them or not, I was getting worried.

I tapped Cleo's box. I tipped Kink's box. I rocked Max's box back and forth. No luck. All they did was peer out at me — one pair of green eyes, one pair of yellow eyes, one pair of furious blue eyes.

"TJ? Are you in here?" My dad looked in the door. "What are you ... ?"

He looked surprised and stepped into the room. Mom peered around the door behind him.

"What's ..." she began. "My goodness, those are the boxes for Gran's cats!"

I told them about my morning phone call.

"Then the cats are in these boxes?" asked Dad.

"Yup," I said. "I'm taking care of them. At least, I will be taking care of them once they come out."

Mom and Dad peered in the boxes.

"Maybe they think they're at the vet's," said my mom.

"Maybe they have Crazy Glue on their feet," said my dad, tipping Kink's box.

"This one looks like it's jammed," said my mom.

She was looking in Max's box. Max truly is a very large cat.

"What about that one?" asked Dad, pointing to the fourth box.

"Escaped," I said.

"In the house?" asked Dad.

"Somewhere," I said.

Right then the phone rang, the doorbell bonged and supper began to burn. Mom and Dad began running around like crazy people again.

I rescued my burnt supper and took

it downstairs to eat in front of the TV. I practiced the things Mom and Dad should have said.

"Taking care of Gran's cats? Why TJ, how responsible of you!"

"You're really growing up, son!"

"And you don't even like cats! Now that's really doing something for your grandmother!"

I figured I might as well practice on myself. No one else seemed to be talking to me.

I stayed in the basement watching TV. The cats stayed in their boxes — they must have come out once or twice because I saw loose crunchies on the floor, but whenever I was in the room they were back in their boxes.

Just before I went to bed I made one last attempt to lure them out. I put out fresh food and water. I tossed their toys around the room. I made all sorts of "kitty, kitty, kitty" noises.

The cats sat in their boxes and stared at me. One pair of green eyes. One pair of yellow eyes. One pair of blue eyes. Cats give me the creeps.

That night I had a nightmare. I dreamed I was in a dark, dark room with a million cat eyes peering at me. I tried to get out but I kept tripping over things. I kept bumping into things. Paint cans. Hardware store shelves. I began to run. This way. That way. I was finding my way to safety. I was sure of it. This way. That way. My feet carried me faster and faster.

But I was finding it harder and harder to breathe. Something was squeezing my chest. I stumbled and fell. The squeezing became a weight upon my chest. The weight became heavier. An enormous rumbling sound filled my ears. I couldn't breathe!

Wake up, I told myself, wake up!

My eyes snapped open. Something *was* pressing heavily on my chest. Its form was dark as midnight, and out of that darkness stared two horrible, glowing eyes — insane, crazed, cat's eyes!

Thump, thump, thump, thump, thump.

There went my heart again.

"Killer?" I whispered hopefully into

the darkness. My voice sounded terrified even to me. "Killer? Is that you?"

It was her all right. She was sitting on my chest, looking into my face and rumbling. It was big rumbling — big and vibrating like giant, earth-eating machinery. I didn't know cats purred like that! It was so strong that I was vibrating too.

I thought hard. If she was purring she must be happy. I didn't want to end up scratched to pieces like the taxi driver. I had to keep her happy.

"Nice kitty," I whispered. "I'm not going to move. Nice kitty."

Killer went on sitting and rumbling. I went on lying there. Even when I felt myself falling asleep again, I willed myself not to move.

In the morning every muscle in my body ached from lying in one place all night. Killer was nowhere to be found.

"You awake, TJ?"

My mom was standing at the door. My mom looks especially nice when I've spent the night with a living nightmare. I would have told her about it too, but she was already pulling on her coat.

"Your lunch is in the fridge. Take care of yourself, okay?"

"Okay," I said.

"And TJ?"

"What?"

"Don't forget about the cats."

Forget about them? How could I forget about them? I'd been tortured by one all night long!

But I almost did forget them. The next time I woke up it was ten minutes until school and I had to run around the house like crazy. It was only at the last minute that I remembered the laundry-room cats. They hadn't made so much as a sound all morning. Maybe they'd stared themselves to death!

I opened the door. All three cats shot out of the room and went galloping down the hall. One ... two ... three ... By the time I followed them into the living room they were nowhere in sight.

I have a theory. Some houses absorb cats. You know the way sponges absorb water? Well that's how some houses are, and ours is one of them. Let a cat loose in our house and — slurp — it's gone.

As I headed down the street to school I had an eerie feeling — a feeling that I was being watched.

Chapter 4

"Listen to this," said Seymour.

We were working on our cat report at the back of the classroom. Seymour was reading and I was writing down notes.

"*When a cat died in ancient Egypt, it was mummified and placed in a jeweled coffin,*" read Seymour. "*The owners shaved their eyebrows to show how sad they were.*"

"They shaved their eyebrows because of a dead cat?" I asked.

Seymour nodded. "I think we should go back to dinosaurs. No one ever ended up with shaved eyebrows because a dinosaur died," he said.

"We're doing cats," I told him. "Look up Sponge Theory."

"What?" asked Seymour.

"See if there's something about cats disappearing."

"Ms. K. doesn't want to hear about the lost-and-found department at the cat pound!" said Seymour. He was waving his hands around again. Amanda was at the front of the room, talking to Ms. K. about her own report, so she didn't have to duck.

"What we need are short and amazing facts," said Seymour. "Tyrannosaurus Rex ate three thousand young children at a single sitting."

"People weren't even around when there were dinosaurs," I said.

"I'm just giving an example," said Seymour. "Here's something good to write down. *Cats can leap five times as high as they are long.*"

"Are you sure that's important?" I asked.

"Can you jump five times as high

as you are long?" asked Seymour.

"No," I said.

"Exactly," said Seymour. "Here's another. *Cats walk on their toes.*"

"Are you sure?" I asked.

"I don't believe it either, but that's what it says," said Seymour. "Here's another. *Cats spend two-thirds of their lives sleeping.*"

"These ideas aren't even related to each other," I said.

"They're all related to cats," said Seymour. "This is a good one. *Cats are strictly carnivores and eat only meat.*" Seymour looked up at me meaningfully.

"I know," I said. "Just like T-Rex."

"Let's change back to dinosaurs," said Seymour. "They didn't spend most of their lives asleep."

"We're doing cats," I said.

Seymour sighed and turned back to the book.

"*A cat's spine is extremely flexible and has more bones than a human spine so cats can bend, twist and climb into cramped spaces.*"

Smack — he closed the book.

"End of report," he said. "You write it out. I'll draw the pictures."

"We can't make a report out of just five facts!" I told Seymour.

"We could if we were doing dinosaurs," said Seymour. "That's how I do it. Every year I use my old report and add five more facts."

"We aren't doing dinosaurs!" I told him for the thousandth time.

"Fine," said Seymour, handing me the books. "You find more facts. I'll draw some pictures."

"Are you going to draw pictures of cats or of dinosaurs?" I asked.

"I haven't decided yet," said Seymour.

I hate doing reports with other people, even if they are my best friends.

The crazy thing is, although I complained about Seymour's "short and amazing facts," I found myself writing down exactly the same sort of thing.

Cats can hear higher and softer sounds than humans can hear.

Mice sounds? Bird sounds?

They have thirty muscles in their ears

to help them locate the source of the sound.

I can't even wiggle my ears.

With a tiny bit of light, cat eyes can see six times better than human eyes.

Great — cats could jump higher, hear better and see in the dark better than I could. Not only did they give me the creeps, I was beginning to feel like a lesser being.

But there was something else about cats' eyes that really did interest me.

Because of an extra layer at the back, cats' eyes reflect light and appear to glow in the dark.

Maybe Killer wasn't insane after all.

I would have read more, but it was time for music. Ms. K. asked us to get out our recorders. Seymour and I took the books back to our desk. He showed me the picture he'd drawn. It was a saber-toothed tiger. I figured he was testing me, so I didn't say anything. With Seymour, things could go either way.

"Did you practice your recorder last night?" asked Seymour.

I shook my head.

"Neither did I," said Seymour glumly. "Ms. K. will ask both of us to play for sure."

He was right of course. Ms. K. knows things. I don't know why we even bother trying to fool her. I made such a mess of my song that I promised myself as soon as I got home I'd practice for eight hours straight, or at least fifteen minutes.

But I didn't.

As soon as I opened our front door my heart began beating like crazy again. Something was very, very wrong.

Chapter 5

It was exactly like they show on those crime programs on TV — robbers had trashed our house! Stuff was thrown everywhere. I'd watched enough crime shows to know not to go inside. I phoned Mom and Dad from the neighbor's house.

Dad drove up ten minutes later. Right behind him came a police car. The police officer went in first. It didn't take her long.

"The thieves are long gone," she said. "If you come in we'll get an idea of what's missing."

The place really was a mess. Garbage, plant parts, dirty laundry, toilet paper — you name it — was spread across the living room and down the halls. How could people do something like that to another person's home?

The funny thing is, nothing was missing. Not the TV. Not the VCR. Not the microwave. Not the money in the cookie tin. It didn't make sense. Didn't we have good enough stuff to be robbed?

The police officer was looking at the sofa. It was covered in toilet paper and plant parts, but there was something else too — clumps of white and orange hair.

"Do you have cats?" she asked suspiciously.

It couldn't be! There hadn't been anything in the library about cats destroying houses.

Just then an orange streak leapt out of nowhere, danced through the plants and disappeared again.

"I'm cat-sitting four of them," I managed to say.

"Four of them!" said the police officer.

She closed her notepad, shook her

head and headed out the door.

I cleaned it up — all of it. I hid the extra toilet paper rolls, found a way to latch the garbage and wedged the potted plants so they wouldn't tip over. It was the least I could do after calling in the entire police force

"It wasn't the entire police force, TJ," said my dad. "And I'm the one who phoned them."

I still felt like an idiot.

Dad decided that since he was home anyway, he'd pack a cold supper. He and Mom could get some extra work done at the store that evening.

"We shouldn't be too late," he said, stopping on his way out the door. "Are you going to be all right, TJ? You look funny. Are you feeling sick?"

Cat sickness, that's what I had. But how could I tell my dad that when he had places to go and things to do?

"I'm okay," I said.

I sat in the living room and watched his car drive away. The house felt quiet and empty all around me. It had felt that way a lot lately, but now it was worse. This time I knew there was something lurking just beneath the silence. Actually there were four somethings.

I had to find the cats. I didn't know what I was going to do when I did, but I had to find them.

I remembered one of Seymour's short and amazing cat facts. *Cats can leap five times as high as they are long.* I stretched out my hands as long as a cat and multiplied the length by five in my head. Those cats could jump almost up to the ceiling!

I began to look up. On top of the fridge? No. On top of the bookshelf?

I climbed on a table and peered over the top of the bookshelf. A pair of emerald green eyes peered back at me from a cloud of gray, white and salmon-colored hair.

"Cleo?" I asked. I don't know why. I knew it was her.

Merow? she asked back at me. It sounded so innocent I felt like gagging.

"Brother," I said.

I climbed back down. I'd found one of the culprits. Where were the others?

Behind me I heard a thump. Cleo had jumped down to the end table. All through the house she followed me as I checked high ledges and shelves.

I had found lots of fur, but no more cats, when Seymour phoned. I knew it was Seymour because who else would play "Hot Cross Buns" on the recorder into the phone?

"All right," I told him. "Hold it. Stop. Cut it out."

"That makes forty-six times," he announced. "I figure that's enough to keep Ms. K.'s witch-radar from locating me for at least a week. Have you practiced yet?"

"No," I said.

"You'd better get started," said Seymour.

He was right.

"And by the way, I took one of the cat books home. I've got a bunch more amazing facts and I've drawn another picture," said Seymour.

I didn't ask him if it was another saber-toothed tiger. I didn't want to take the chance.

After I hung up I got my recorder. I sat on the living-room floor and spread my music in front of me. Cleo sat on my music.

"Cleo, get off!" I said. I reached out to pull the music away.

Cleo yawned – a yawn that showed many sharp teeth.

She stretched – a stretch that sent sharp, curved claws pulling at the carpet.

I figured I could play from memory.

Hot cross buns. Hot cross buns. One a penny, two a penny, Hot cross buns.

Cleo blinked at me and began to groom herself. Lick. Lick. The music wasn't perfect, but one or two of the notes were right. I tried again.

Hot cross buns. Hot cross buns. One a p ...

I stopped playing. Something was wrong. I could hear it. I could see it too. It was spooky, but it was happening — our sofa was moving!

Thump, thump, thump, thump, thump.

There went my heart again. The way my life was going lately, if I didn't drown I was going to die of a heart attack.

Chapter 6

Be calm. Be cool. Don't panic. DON'T call the police.

Our sofa moving? Naw. Sofas don't move. It was my imagination.

Hot cross buns. Hot cross buns. One a p ...

The sofa *was* moving. One of the cushions was lifting. A pair of orange ears, a pair of yellow eyes and a hairy orange body were squeezing out from beneath the cushions. Kink! He'd been right inside the frame of the sofa!

Halfway in and halfway out, Kink stopped and looked at me. He was bent and twisted but didn't seem bothered.

I remembered another of Seymour's amazing cat facts.

A cat's spine is extremely flexible and has more bones than a human spine.

There was a scrabbling sound and Kink used his back feet to push himself free.

"Did you know he was there?" I asked Cleo.

Merow, she replied. It sounded like "Yes, you silly twit."

Kink sat on the sofa. Cleo sat on my music. They both seemed to be waiting for something. I went back to playing.

Hot cross buns. Hot cross buns. One a p ...

Reow! said Kink. He leapt from the sofa and ran stiff-legged towards me. He began to bunt and push at my recorder with his head.

"What are you doing, you dumb cat?"

Bunt, bunt. Push, push.

I played a few notes on the recorder.

Bunt, bunt. Push, push. *Prrrrrrrrrrrrr.*

I finished my practice with Cleo licking herself on my music and Kink purring and bunting in my lap. Why on earth had I wanted to find the cats anyway?

Suddenly Cleo began to make noise of her own.

Gargumph. Gargumph.

Her whole body began to ripple and heave.

Gargumph. Gagarumph.

Panic gripped me. A cat was going into death spasms right in front of me. What was I supposed to do?

Gargumph. Gargumph.

I grabbed the phone. I dialed Seymour's number.

"Get the cat books," I told him. "Look up death throes. Look up fits. Look up ... gakking!"

"What?" said Seymour.

That's the sound Cleo was making now.

Gak. Gak. GAK!

With a final heave of her body she coughed up something lumpy on my music.

"Barfing!" I shouted into the phone. "Look up barfing!"

"No," said Seymour. "That's disgusting."

"Seymour, if you ever want to be my friend for the rest of your entire life you'll look it up!" I said.

"You're nuts," he said. "No book is going to have the word 'barfing' in it. And why do you want to know anyway?"

He was right. There had to be another word. Gagging. Up-chucking.

"Vomiting!" I yelled.

"All right. Don't shout," said Seymour. "Vomiting is in the index. Now what?"

"Read it," I said.

"Sure. Why not? I love to read about cats vomiting."

"Just read it, Seymour."

I could hear him flipping to the right page.

"*Cats often vomit to get rid of hair balls.*" Seymour paused. "Do I have to keep reading this stuff?"

"Yes," I said.

"You owe me," said Seymour. "*Hair balls are made from swallowed hair and* — oh yuck! — *partly digested food.*"

"Keep reading," I said.

"*Hair balls are harmless and can*

be avoided by brushing long-haired cats every day," read Seymour.

Harmless. Relief swept over me.

"That's good," I said. "Thanks."

"Don't you want to hear more?" asked Seymour. "There are pages and pages about cats vomiting."

"I'll call you back if I need more," I said and hung up.

Gritting my teeth, I looked closely at what Cleo had left on my music. Yup, it was made of hair and something that might once have been food. I took a deep breath, picked up the music, hurried down the hall and tipped the hair ball into the toilet.

Cleo and Kink followed me. Kink sat on the toilet tank and peered into the toilet. Closer and closer he peered. It was like he was watching TV in the toilet bowl. There was definitely something strange about Kink, and it wasn't just his tail.

Suddenly he jumped straight up, did a double twist off the tank and raced into the hall. Cleo bounded after him. What was going on?

Two minutes later the front door opened and Mom and Dad came in. Had the cats known they were coming? Did they have ESP? Or did cats have such good hearing they could hear a car turn the corner down at the end of the street?

"Sorry we're so late, TJ," said my mom.

"Boy, am I beat," said my dad. "Did you have any more trouble with the cats?"

They both really did look exhausted. I figured they didn't want to hear about ESP, toilet watching and hair balls.

"Not much," I said.

"Good grief," said my mom behind us.

If my mom's had a rough day she soaks her feet in a roasting pan she keeps in the bottom cupboard. Max was sitting in the roasting pan.

"Do you suppose he thinks he's a turkey or a goose?" asked my mom.

"Looks like a turkey to me," said my dad.

It was a pretty good line, but neither

of them laughed. People who take over hardware stores lose their sense of humor entirely.

"I need this roasting pan more than you do, cat," said my mom.

She tipped the roasting pan slowly up and down. For a while Max went up and down with it. On the eighth tip or so he must have begun to get the idea. Either that or he began to get seasick.

He stepped out of the roasting pan, walked across the kitchen floor and sat by another cupboard door. He reached out a paddy paw. Bat. Bat. The door bounced ajar. Max walked in.

I checked on him just before I went to bed. He was sitting in a frying pan.

Chapter 7

"Boy, do you look awful," said Seymour when I got to school the next morning.

"I feel awful," I told him.

I was crabby. I was sore. I felt like I'd been dragged around the living room and run over by a herd of cats.

Cleo had lain beside me on the bed and pushed. I don't sleep well on the very edge of the bed.

Kink had played midnight hockey with a bottle cap on my bedroom floor — *thwack, scrabble-scrabble, thwack.* I can't sleep with someone playing hockey on my bedroom floor.

And then there was that awful feeling

of drowning. Panic and drowning. Why did I keep thinking of that sailor going under for the third time? What was wrong with me?

At least I knew not to panic as badly when Killer arrived with her glowing eyes at midnight. They only glowed when the hall light caught them at a certain angle. Those eyes weren't madness; they were science. Everything was science.

"Do you want to hear my new and amazing cat facts?" asked Seymour.

Seymour was really beginning to get into the report. That's the way Seymour is.

"Sure," I said.

"*Each cat's nose print is unique*," read Seymour, "*like our fingerprints. Neat, eh?*"

"I guess so," I said. "How do people know these things?"

"They make them up," said Seymour.

"They do?" I asked.

"Just kidding," said Seymour. "They must have some sort of harmless kind of ink they use. Here's another. *Cats kill with a sharp bite to the neck.*"

That was gruesome, but interesting. Gran's cats were indoor cats — even Cleo, who had been adopted as a young stray two months ago. It made you forget that all this leaping, batting, clawing, see-in-the-dark stuff was because cats were made to hunt and kill. Carnivores. If you were a carnivore in the wild you didn't pick up cat crunchies at the grocery store.

"Did you read about how cats purr?" I asked.

"I found lots of theories — bones vibrating at the base of the tongue, blood rushing through the big vessels in a cat's chest." Seymour checked his notes. "*Newest research suggests that cats can move their vocal chords so quickly that a vibrating column of air in the throat sounds as a purr and is just the right frequency to set the cat's entire body vibrating. That's why you can feel by touching that the cat is purring.*"

I preferred my own Big Machinery Theory. It had the same kind of catchiness as my Sponge Theory.

"Here's another fact," said Seymour. "*When cats sit in the sun and groom themselves they are also licking vitamin D that forms on their fur.*"

"How can vitamins form on cat fur?" I asked.

"Here's the book. Read about it for yourself," said Seymour. "Here are my pictures."

The first one was a mummified cat. The second was a cat coffin.

"I tried to draw some live cats too," said Seymour.

This time the drawings looked like dinosaurs with fur. I didn't say that, of course, but Seymour and I have been friends a long time and sometimes he reads my mind.

"I didn't make them look like dinosaurs on purpose," said Seymour. "They just keep coming out that way."

I turned the picture upside down. Nope, it didn't look any better. It didn't look any worse either. I looked at the book from which he'd copied.

"I'm good at dinosaurs because I've been to the museum to see them so many times," said Seymour. "Maybe if there was a cat museum or something ..."

Seymour kept talking, but I wasn't listening. I'd gone from looking at pictures of cats to reading what was written underneath. It was a whole page about cats and people and how they get along together. It was clicking on all sorts of little lights in my brain and making me feel a lot better. It was making me feel so much better that I decided to take a chance.

"Look," I said to Seymour, "why don't you come over to my place after school? I've got something better than a cat museum. Actually it's better and worse all at once."

"What is it?" asked Seymour.

"Just something," I said.

Of course he couldn't leave it at "just something."

"What is it?" he asked me all through math.

"What is it?" he asked all through science.

In music, where Ms. K. didn't ask

us to play because she knew we'd practiced, Seymour asked for the two hundredth time.

"What is it?"

Amanda looked across at me hopefully. It's not easy for her, sitting behind Seymour all day.

But I didn't tell him. I wasn't sure what he'd say and anyway, I wanted it to be a surprise.

Chapter 8

"Cats!" said Seymour, looking around our kitchen. "You've got cats!"

Cleo was peeking over the top of the refrigerator.

Kink was playing paddy-ball with something under the stove.

Huge, gigantic Max had tried to stuff himself into a tissue box on the counter and had flattened it completely.

As we stood there, a small black shadow made a quick dart down from a chair to streak along the hall — Killer's first daytime appearance.

"Where'd they come from? Where'd

you get them? What are their names?"

Seymour can ask a lot of questions when he gets going.

"Are they all yours? Is this why you wanted to do the cat report? Why didn't you ..." He paused to sniff. "Why didn't you tell me?"

"I'm cat-sitting them for two weeks as a favor to my Gran," I said. "I'm an ailurophobe, so it's kind of tricky."

"A what?" asked Seymour.

"An ailurophobe," I said. "Cats give me the creeps."

That's what I'd read in Seymour's book. An ailurophobe can be someone who hates cats or someone who has an unexplained fear of cats. It was the last part that really interested me. Now I understood that feeling of panic and drowning. Giving it a long name like *ailurophobia* made it seem okay to feel that way.

"Since you don't like cats, you're probably an ailurophobe too," I said.

"Not me," said Seymour. "I'm just allergic."

I looked at him. His eyes were watering like crazy and he was sniffing for about the eighth time. Cleo and Kink began to rub back and forth against his legs.

"I've got to get out of here," said Seymour.

Out the front he went. As the door closed, I felt let down. It had been fun, just for a minute, to have someone else to talk to about the cats.

I didn't have time to feel sorry for myself. Max walked up and bit me in the ankle. He didn't draw blood, but it was a bite all right.

"Max!"

He bit me again.

"Max! Cut it out!"

Cleo began to meow up at me. Was she going to bite me too?

Suddenly Kink exploded. In a tremendous burst of energy he tore around the kitchen, raced down the hall to the laundry room and flew back to the kitchen again.

I was hit with a flash of understanding. Something was wrong. Cats were like all those dogs on TV shows that try to warn people. My heart began to pound.

"Okay," I said.

The cats sensed that I was now on their side. Cleo and Kink bounded ahead of me down the hall. Max nipped at my heels.

They herded me into the laundry room. I expected to find Killer laid out with a heart attack or a hole in the wall where the dryer had blown up. Instead I found something much worse. It was so awful all three of them began to howl wretchedly.

The terrible truth was — their food bowls were empty.

Their food bowls were empty! No wonder there's a special word like *ailurophobia*. Cats drive a person crazy!

I fed them. I watered them. I tried to ignore what was sitting at the other end of the laundry room, but I couldn't. Things were getting just too smelly.

I used to think cleaning my room was the worst job in the world. It's not. Cleaning the kitty litter for four cats is the most disgusting, revolting job in the world. Only for the world's greatest Gran would I do something like clean out a tray of dirty kitty litter.

Mom and Dad came home late. When they did arrive it was like a hurricane again. The phone rang, laundry flew, food burned and all Mom and Dad wanted to talk about was the store.

I copied the cats. I found myself a place to hide and stayed there until bedtime.

Chapter 9

The cats developed a routine.

In the mornings Max stared at my cereal bowl while I ate. I left a few drops of milk in the bowl and set it on the floor for him. Maybe I was the one who was developing a routine.

When I came home at lunch, Cleo wanted me to pet her. I used the brush and cut down on the hair ball index at the same time.

After school, Kink did his special thing. He exploded. He burst out of paper bags, attacked my feet and ran around the house like a whole herd of cats. I cleaned up after him as best I could.

At night, between bouts of midnight hockey or general prowling, all four of them climbed on and off the bed to sleep with me. Cleo slept on one side. Kink slept on the other. Max slept across my feet. Killer slept on my chest. Sometimes I felt like a hot dog in a furry bun. It was a true test of willpower for an ailurophobe, especially since there was a good deal of growling and hissing as they protected their sleeping spots. It's not easy to sleep beneath a blanket of fighting cats. Every morning I felt like I'd been through a war zone.

Seymour, meanwhile, was really getting into cats. He'd asked his mom about allergy medicine so he could come and study them in person. He'd found a book about cats and disasters. Seymour loves disasters.

"Hurricanes, volcanoes, earthquakes — cats have warned people about them all," Seymour told me. "They have some kind of sense that tells them when a disaster is coming. Sometimes it can be explained by the way cats are so sensitive to sound and vibrations, but not all the time. Cats *know* things."

"Kind of like Ms. K.," I said.

That morning Ms. K. had told me that growing boys need more than three hours of sleep a night. How did she know that's all I was getting?

"Cats even know directions," said Seymour. "If you take a cat away from home in a closed box and put it in a maze, it still knows how to get back home."

That's all I needed, another nightmare about cats and mazes. I still hadn't found where Killer hid out during the day.

"And there's one really weird thing, but it's hard to prove," said Seymour. "It's called psi-trailing. A person moves and the cat gets left behind. Months later, the cat shows up on the owner's *new* doorstep, even though it's never been anywhere near that house before. Even Ms. K. can't do that — not without an address anyway."

"I wouldn't count on it," I said.

Ms. K. had written *How are your four feline friends?* on the bottom of my math homework. She knew we were doing a cat report, but I hadn't told her I was living with four of them. How could she have known?

"Cats have helped rescue people from floods, car accidents, fires ..."

Seymour was interrupted by Ms. K. calling the class to attention.

"We'll be starting the science report presentations next week," she announced. "Would anyone be ready for Monday?"

Amanda's hand shot into the air.

"I can be ready," said Amanda, "but I'll need four more sheets of poster paper and could I use the computer and two tables and the slide projector?"

When class let out, Seymour was more upset than I'd seen him in a long time.

"Four sheets of poster paper, the computer, two tables and the slide projector!"

I understood. Every year when it's time to do reports, Amanda does the best one of the class. Usually she goes a little overboard and our report ends up looking just a little pathetic next to hers. With the list of equipment she'd given Ms. K., however, this year there could be real trouble. Seymour pretends he doesn't care, but the truth is he likes to do good reports — even if they are always about dinosaurs.

We headed downtown. On Friday afternoons Seymour and I buy slushies and then stop at the store. It had been neat to do when the store first opened. My parents' hardware store has all sorts of good things like camping gear and baseball equipment. Today, however, walking around looking at what was on the shelves seemed pretty point-less. Nothing in the hardware store actually belonged to us. It was all there to be sold to other people.

Seymour was restless and he headed home. He was still thinking about Amanda and the science reports. I hung around getting more and more rest-less myself. Finally I took some washable markers and began drawing mustaches on all those smiling people whose photos get put in empty picture frames so customers will want to buy them.

I'd just given a blonde lady a long blue beard when I looked up. Ms. K. was walking towards me. I put the frames back and stood in front of them.

"Do you know where your mom and dad keep the motor oil, TJ?" she asked.

"Sure," I said.

Except I didn't. The car section was all mixed up and I had to walk around and around the store like a real jerk before I found it.

But the worst part was that when I carried the two quarts of oil to the till for Ms. K., my dad came up waving something in his hand.

"Some rotten kid has made a real mess of these," he announced. He set the picture frames on the counter in front of Mom and Ms. K. and everyone else. The blue marker was still in my hand, and if I stood there even two seconds longer they were all going to figure out who the rotten kid was.

I had to get out of there. And I had

to get out fast. Suddenly I remembered I had the perfect excuse.

"I forgot about the cats! I've got to go home and feed them," I exclaimed and hurried out of the store.

Maybe Seymour was right about cats saving people from disasters after all.

Chapter 10

"TJ, why are you still in your pyjamas?" asked my mom the next day. It was almost noon. She'd come home to pick up lunch and take me down to the store. That's what she always did on Saturday afternoons.

"I'm not coming to the store," I said.

"Why not?" asked my mom.

"Hardwareaphobia," I said.

"Hardware-a-what?" asked my mom.

"Hardwareaphobia," I said. "Fear and dislike of hardware stores."

"Oh dear," began my mom, sitting beside me on the sofa. "What's wrong, TJ?"

"Nothing's wrong," I said. I slid down to the other end of the sofa. "I just have it, that's all — hardwareaphobia. I even had a hardware store nightmare last week."

My mom looked at me silently for a moment.

"So you're not coming," she said.

"Nope," I said.

I thought maybe my mom would yell at me or order me to come or phone Dad. She didn't. She frowned, but she didn't say anything.

I didn't feel very good after she left. Mom and Dad had always dreamed of having their own business and they were working really hard to make it successful. I knew that. I hadn't meant to make her feel bad about it — I just really didn't want to be there. And to tell you the truth, I hadn't even known what I was going to say until I opened my mouth and the words came tumbling out.

"Does that ever happen to you?" I asked Max.

He didn't answer.

Max was sitting on my lap. So long as he was awake it was fine, but after a while he'd fall asleep. Sleeping cats weigh a lot more than cats that are awake. Max was up to about the weight of an elephant when Seymour phoned.

"Why aren't you at the store?" he asked.

"Because," I said.

"Glad you explained it to me," said Seymour. "I'll be over as soon as I take my allergy medicine and find a tin of tuna."

The allergy medicine was so Seymour wouldn't get all stuffed up. The tuna was so he could lure Killer out of hiding.

Of course he lured the three other cats as well. Around and around the house he went with the open tin and three cats meowing and howling on his heels. Finally Seymour put half the contents of the tin on a plate in the kitchen for the three howlers.

"Where does Killer show up at night?" asked Seymour.

"My room," I said.

We went into my bedroom and closed the door. Seymour held the open tuna tin on high. After a few moments we heard a small sound at the top of my closet. I hadn't even tried to search there because it was such a mess.

We looked up. A small, black, pointy thing was moving ever so slightly above the lumps of junk. A moment later we could see a bit of fur and a second black, pointy thing. At last two amazing copper eyes looked down on us like glowing pennies. It was Killer all right.

We set the tuna on the bed and waited. Killer dropped from the top of my closet to my bed. She walked cautiously up to the dish and began to eat.

"I don't think she's a killer at all," said Seymour. "I think she's just nervous."

"Gran might have called her Killer to give her confidence," I said. "Gran does things like that. Why did you want her?"

"I read another neat book about cats last night," said Seymour. "You know how black cats and witches go together?"

"Maybe," I said. I hoped he wasn't

thinking of putting Ms. K. into our cat report.

"Well, in the Dark Ages, people who were thought to be witches were burned at the stake — and so were black cats," said Seymour.

"That's awful!" I said.

"So many black cats were killed that it practically wiped them out. According to the book, most black cats today have at least a tiny bit of white on them. I want to check Killer and see if it's true."

We checked Killer's fur. On her chest was a tiny cluster of white hairs that formed a very small star.

"There was something weird about white cats too," said Seymour. "Where's Max?"

Max was waiting just outside the door, hoping for more tuna.

"White cats with blue eyes are deaf," said Seymour. "At least a lot of them are."

"That doesn't make any sense," I said. "What does hair color have to do with eyes?"

"It's something called genetics," said

Seymour. "Cats like Cleo with three colors on their coats are female. And white cats with blue eyes ..."

"Max," I said, bending down to him, "if you can hear me, meow twice."

"Come on," said Seymour. "This is really true. Walk up behind him and make noise."

I walked behind Max, shouted "Yaaaaaahhh!" and stomped on the floor like crazy. Max took off like a shot. All the cats took off like shots. Seymour frowned at me and shook his head.

"What's wrong?" I asked.

"I said deaf, not dead," said Seymour. "Don't stomp — you shook the whole house. Don't even clap your hands — it moves air currents and cats' whiskers can feel it. Their paddy paws feel vibrations too, so you'd better be really careful walking up behind him."

Seymour was turning into a regular cat encyclopedia.

"Creep up and then just give a little yell," he said.

Max and Cleo were both in the living room. Cleo was pacing back and forth restlessly at the window. She'd started to do that lately. Max was washing himself. His back was to me. Very slowly I walked across the carpet. I waited a few moments.

"Boo!" I said.

Cleo's head turned instantly, but Max just kept cleaning himself.

"Boo! Yahhhhhh! Whoooo!"

I made high sounds. I made low sounds. Max just kept cleaning himself. Seymour was right. Most cats may have great ears, but this one could hear about as well as a rock.

"I wish we could test some of the other things, like direction-finding or psi-trailing," said Seymour.

"If you think I'm going to let them out so we can see if they can find Gran in Hawaii, forget it," I said. "They'd have to swim, for crying out loud!"

Seymour was gone by the time Mom and Dad got home. That was just as well, because I could tell they were pretty upset with me for not coming to the store. They didn't say anything, but that almost made it worse. I think even Cleo felt the tension. She began to howl and seemed to be asking at the door to go out.

"Before I forget to tell you, TJ, the furnace cleaners are coming next Wednesday," said my mom. "You better put the cats in the laundry room for the day."

She didn't even look at me when she said it.

"Right," I said.

At that moment, Wednesday seemed a long way off.

Chapter 11

All Sunday Seymour and I worked like crazy. We organized, we typed, we drew, we made posters. The cats helped us. They sat on our poster paper. They rolled our markers off the table. They played hockey with our glue stick. They walked through the houseplants and left smudgy black cat tracks over everything.

The only one that didn't come out to sit on our posters or knock our pens off the table was Killer. Killer was still very shy. Every night, however, she sat on my chest.

She was there the night the police came. Three in the morning is when they came, and it was their siren that woke us all up. The doorbell rang, and before Mom or Dad could get to the door, I could hear someone trying the handle.

"We had a 9-1-1 call from this address," the officer said as Dad opened the door.

"From here?" asked Mom. "No one phoned from here."

I think I figured it out at the same moment as the police officer. She wasn't happy about it.

"Aren't you the people with the problem cats?" she asked.

We went into the living room. The phone was off the hook all right. There were cat hairs drifting all around it.

"But how could a cat dial 9-1-1?" Mom asked.

"The memory buttons," said Dad.

We apologized about a hundred times to the police officer and turned off all the memory buttons on the phone.

"They probably hit number 4 and ordered pizza while they were at it," said Dad as he and Mom headed back to bed.

"So long as they didn't hit number 5 and phone your brother in Alaska," said Mom.

I decided not to mention I'd found the phone off the hook at least four times in the last few days.

Seymour thought the cats calling 9-1-1 was a hoot.

"I bet the police have a big black X next to your address," he said. "Even if your house is burning they won't come unless you can prove it's not a cat lighting matches."

"Ha, ha," I said. Between the police and the cats I'd had even less sleep than usual.

"Maybe we could use it for our report," Seymour went on. "The police officer could come in and talk about criminal cats."

"Seymour!"

"All right, but Amanda's next up. From the amount of stuff I saw her carrying to school, I think she's really gone nuts this time," said Seymour.

Seymour was right about her going overboard. She had all sorts of things to set up that afternoon. But even worse was her topic — dinosaurs.

"Dinosaurs!" hissed Seymour at me across the aisle. "She's supposed to do porcupines!"

"I guess she changed her mind," I said.

"She can't do that!" said Seymour.

"We did," I told him.

"You're the one who changed your mind," said Seymour. "I just went along with it. That doesn't mean I gave up dinosaurs."

"Tell Amanda," I said.

"I can't tell Amanda! You know what she's like!" said Seymour.

What Amanda is like is nice. She's so nice that when Seymour waves his arms around or asks a million questions, she doesn't get mad at him unless he's really out of line.

She had done a lot of work. She had charts. She had posters. She had slides, overheads, models and plaster footprints. She even had a computer program, for crying out loud.

"What a disaster," moaned Seymour when it was over.

"I'm sorry I made you give up dinosaurs," I said.

"I don't think it would have made any difference," said Seymour.

And that's all he said. Seymour, who talks a mile a minute, was silent all the way to my place. That's how depressed he was.

Seymour went home. I went in the house and flopped on the sofa. Max flopped on top of me and proceeded to gain weight. Kink rubbed back and forth on the floor under my dangling arm until I petted him. Cleo paced restlessly back and forth across the top of the sofa and shed long hairs down on me. Even Killer showed up, still shy, peering out from a hiding place in the plants.

I had to admit that I was feeling pretty down in the dumps. Seymour had managed to draw some good pictures. We had all sorts of neat facts. We'd done a good poster. Next to Amanda's presentation, however, it was all going to seem completely dull.

Cats weren't dull! They were annoying, weird, unpredictable and drove a person crazy — but they weren't dull!

Suddenly I sat bolt upright. Cats went flying north, south and center. I reached for the phone.

"Seymour," I said when he answered, "there's something Amanda didn't do."

"Yeah, right," said Seymour. "She didn't shoot off fireworks and she didn't show up with T-Rex under her arm."

"Exactly," I said. "Especially the last part."

I would have liked to see him then. I know what it's like when that good old light comes back into Seymour's eyes.

I felt so good about my brain wave that I couldn't sit still after I got off the phone. I had to do something. It didn't have to be something to do with cats; it just had to be *something*. I baked my favorite batch of cookies. And then, because being in the kitchen made me hungrier and hungrier, I made macaroni and cheese from a package and threw all the leftovers from the fridge into it. I'd got the idea from a TV commercial, but that didn't matter — it might just work. By the time Mom and Dad came home I'd even set the table.

I didn't expect them to be as surprised as they were. They just stood there.

"I'm starving," I said. "Let's eat."

"I've no objections," said Dad. "It doesn't even smell burnt."

Of course as soon as they sat down, the telephone rang. Mom walked over to it and pulled the cord out of its jack. Mom doesn't usually do things like that. Dad and I looked at her in shock.

"Stare all you like," said Mom, sitting down to her meal. "I don't know why things just got better around here, but they did and I'm going to see it lasts another ten minutes at least."

It lasted longer than ten minutes. Dad asked me why I'd cooked supper, and I started talking about being in a good mood because of the cat report. Pretty soon I was telling them all sorts of things — cat facts, Seymour facts, stories about Max and Cleo and Kink and Killer.

"I didn't realize you'd been through so much with those cats," said my mom.

"I didn't even think you liked cats," said my dad. "In fact, I thought you always avoided them at Gran's house."

"We *all* avoided them at Gran's house," said my mom.

"Ailurophobia," I said. "That's what it's called when cats give you the creeps."

"Ailurophobia," said my mom. Then she gave an odd little half smile. "Kind of like hardwareaphobia."

Dad had stopped eating and was watching me across the table.

"But you got over it?" he asked. "You got over this ailurophobia?"

"I had to," I said. "The cats needed me."

It was as if something in the room shifted then. Dad sighed. Mom became very, very quiet.

"TJ," said Mom softly, "we don't very often tell you this, but we need you too."

"We don't get to see you much these

days. We miss you," said Dad.

"That's why we like it when you visit us down at the store," said Mom. "It makes us feel like we're still a family."

I hadn't thought about them missing me at the store as much as I missed them around home.

"But all I do there is hang around looking dumb," I said.

"Would it help if you had a job?" asked Dad. "Would that help you get over the hardwareaphobia?"

"It might," I said. "But not some sort of made-up job for little kids that doesn't count. I can handle more than some dumb job for little kids."

Dad looked over his shoulder at Kink, Cleo, Max and Killer spread across the dining-room floor like area rugs — happy, contented area rugs.

"Yes," he said, "I think you can handle a lot more than we've been giving you credit for. Let your mom and me think on it a bit."

Chapter 12

That night I had the best sleep I'd had in a long time, in spite of being surrounded by furry bodies. In the morning I felt a thousand times better, plus Seymour and I were pretty excited about the possibility of bringing a live exhibit for our report.

"Only one cat, and bring it after lunch tomorrow, please," said Ms. K.

I couldn't believe it. We hadn't even asked. All we'd done was walk up to her desk with our best smiles on our faces. Ms. K. really does know things.

Seymour and I walked home at lunch on Wednesday and carried Kink to school in his fun-house box. Our class sat in a circle with the cat box in the middle. Seymour opened the door. No cat came out, but we were ready. I took out my recorder.

Hot cross buns, hot cross buns,
Kink peered out of the carry-box.
one a-penny, two a-penny,
Kink took a step forward.
hot, cross buns.
Kink bounded into my lap.

A quiet ripple of laughter went around the circle. Kink looked around. He was in the center of a show ring. Maybe this wasn't so bad!

Hot cross buns, hot cross buns
Seymour was playing on the other side of the circle. Kink looked at him, merowed happily, and walked in his funny dancing way over to rub against Seymour's recorder. Seymour beamed.

Kids began to talk to Kink and call him. Several had their own cats at home, of course, but it was still fun for them to have a cat in class. It was also neat to be able to look at a cat while Seymour and I took turns reading our report. It was easy to show things like the way

cats really do walk on their toes, the way their ears move, the shape of their eyes.

Kink liked being the center of attention. He liked it so much, in fact, that he began to step higher and higher. All of a sudden I knew what was coming next.

"I think maybe he should go back now," I said.

It was too late. Kink had one of his explosions. He leaped high out of the circle, raced three times around the room, skidded through the papers on Ms. K.'s desk, knocked all the brushes off the chalkboard, tore three posters off the bulletin board and came to a stop on the filing cabinet. There he sat grooming himself as if nothing at all out of the usual had happened.

"I'm not here," I told Seymour, ducking behind him.

"It's okay," he said. "The room's a mess, but Ms. K.'s smiling."

It was true. She *was* smiling.

"You may return to your desks now, class," said Ms. K. "It's time for math."

All through the math lesson Kink

sat on the filing cabinet. He looked like he was trying to learn division. Just before the final bell rang, Ms. K. walked over and rubbed him behind the ears.

"Kink," said Ms. K., "back in your house, please."

She motioned toward the box on the floor. Kink jumped off the cabinet, crossed to his carry-box and walked in.

"In the Dark Ages she'd have been burned at the stake for getting a cat to obey her that way," said Seymour as we filed out of class.

But he wasn't complaining. Our report, complete with living exhibit, had been a wonderful success. Even Amanda had said so. And besides, there are times when it's neat having a teacher who's a witch.

I only wish she could have warned us what was going on at home at that very moment.

Chapter 13

The cats were gone.

As soon as we walked into the house we felt it. They weren't just hiding in the sofa or on top of the bookcase — they were gone.

"The furnace cleaners!" I said. "The furnace cleaners were coming today! How could I have forgotten?"

"What door do they use?" asked Seymour.

"The back," I said.

He was already hurrying through the house.

Off we went into the backyard, calling the cats, "Cleo! Max! Killer!"

"We'd better split up," said Seymour.

Seymour went one way up the alley. I went the other way. How could I have forgotten?

Just as I came around onto the street, I heard a wonderful sound.

Meeeeeeow!

Killer was perched in an apple tree, looking worriedly down at me with her copper-penny eyes. She really was a scaredy-cat. I climbed up on a fence beside the tree, detached her claws one by one from the bark and lifted her down.

I walked back towards the house. Seymour was coming from the other direction. There was something big and white in his arms. Hurrah!

"I found him sitting in the middle of the road," said Seymour as we went up the walk together. "Talk about a dumb place for a deaf cat to sit."

Just the thought of what might have happened made me feel sick inside. How could I have forgotten about the furnace cleaners coming?

Cats! Cats! Catscatscatscats!

The dog next door was rushing the

house. Instantly I was covered in cat hair. That's what Killer does when she panics — she sheds. And then she became a hysterical hurricane of claws and armpits clawing her way to the highest point she could reach at that moment — my head. Now I knew how the taxi driver had felt.

I raced the last few steps and threw open our door. Killer leaped for safety. I turned back to help Seymour.

Max was sitting placidly in Seymour's arms. Seymour had turned him around so he couldn't see either the dog or Killer's panic. Max was blissfully ignorant.

"I like this cat," said Seymour, and carried him into the house.

Kink was safe in his cat box. Killer had fled to the safety of my closet. Max was safe in Seymour's arms. But Cleo was missing.

We scoured the neighborhood. We knocked on doors. We talked to everyone on the street. We set out tins of tuna that attracted every other cat around.

But we didn't find Cleo.

That night Mom let me phone Gran in Hawaii.

"Gran?" I said when I heard her voice on the phone. I could almost picture my awful news traveling all those long, lonely miles across the ocean to reach her. "I'm really sorry. I've let you down. Cleo's missing."

"Oh dear," said Gran.

"I'm really, really sorry. I'll keep looking. I'd do anything to get her back. It's all my fault," I said.

"Cleo, did you say?" asked Gran. "Oh dear."

"Gran, are you all right? You haven't fainted or anything have you?"

"No, no," said Gran. "I'm just thinking. Now listen, TJ This isn't all your fault. I'm to blame too. I'd been meaning to take Cleo to see the veterinarian ever since I adopted her, but I kept putting it off. If I'd taken her when I should have she wouldn't have run away. Oh my."

I didn't understand what she meant about the vet, but I didn't like to ask.

It was my fault Cleo was missing and I didn't want to duck any of the blame.

"Well, TJ," said Gran. "We'll just have to wait and see."

Chapter 14

For three days, in every spare moment, we looked for Cleo.

Mom checked Gran's house and phoned the animal shelter. Dad handed out lost cat flyers at the store. Seymour and I walked miles around every place we thought a cat could possibly want to go. By the time evening rolled around on Saturday we were exhausted. We ate supper and collapsed in the middle of the living room. Max, Killer and Kink collapsed around us. They weren't tired, but they collapsed anyway. Cats are like that. They also seemed totally content.

"I don't think they even know she's gone," I said.

"Cats walk alone," said my dad. "That's an old saying."

"Does that mean she's never coming back?" I asked my dad.

"I don't know," Dad answered. "I wish I had a crystal ball that I could look into and tell you where to find her."

"It's funny," said Mom. "It used to annoy me when Cleo sat on the newspaper when I wanted to read it. This morning I looked at the paper and wished she *was* sitting on it."

"I found myself leaving the tap on so she could play in the drips after I'd finished shaving," said Dad. "I didn't think cats like water, but Cleo did."

"Kink likes it too, especially staring into the toilet bowl," said Mom. "And have you noticed how Max stuffs himself into things? I found him in a shoe box this morning."

Mom and Dad kept talking about the cats, but I was way back at the beginning, the part about the crystal ball.

I was desperate. Really desperate. Gran would be home tomorrow. Maybe a little crystal ball magic really would work. But was I brave enough to ask?

I decided to take Seymour along for extra support.

"You can't just go knocking on Ms. K.'s door out of nowhere on a Saturday night!" said Seymour on our way over to her house. "What are you going to tell her? What if she flunks you for losing something you did a report on? She can't really be a witch!"

Ms. K. herself opened the door. I just stood there. Seymour was right. What was I going to say?

"Hi!" I said.

"Hello, TJ. Hello, Seymour," said Ms. K.

"Nice evening," I said.

"It is," said Ms. K.

"Might rain," I said.

"It might," said Ms. K.

"Might not," I said.

"Then again it might not," said Ms. K.

She wasn't making it easy for me. I took a deep breath.

"I've come because I was hoping you could find Cleo for me," I said. "She's my Gran's cat. She's got green eyes and fluffy fur and she's gray and white and salmon-colored and I thought maybe you'd know where she was or could figure it out. If you didn't mind trying. Please."

Ms. K. frowned.

"Why are you asking me, TJ?" she asked. "Are you knocking on everyone's door?"

"No," I said.

"Then why me?"

I could have said it was because I knew her. I could have said it was because Seymour told me to. I could have said it was because I'd gone totally insane. Instead I told her the truth. Well, not exactly. I told her as close to the truth as I dared admit. Even I know not to tell a teacher she's a witch.

"Because you *know* things," I said.

Ms. K. looked even more puzzled.

"What do you mean?" she asked.

"Things," I said. "Like when Seymour and I haven't practiced our recorders."

Ms. K. smiled.

"You and Seymour always make faces at each other at the start of music class if you haven't practiced," she said.

"We do?" asked Seymour.

"And the way you knew about us wanting to bring the cats to class," I said.

"I heard you talking about it all the way down the hall," said Ms. K. "Seymour's voice gets pretty loud when he's excited."

"It does?" asked Seymour.

"But what about when you wrote on my math homework about four feline friends?" I said.

"There were cat hairs all over the pages — long ones, short ones, black ones, white ones ..." said Ms. K. "I figured about four cats for that many different types of hair."

"Then ..." I could feel my heart sinking down to my toes. Ms. K. had been my last hope. "Then you can't tell me where Cleo is?"

"That's the strange part of all this," said Ms. K. "I can't figure out how you thought to come here. Maybe you're the one who knows things, TJ"

Ms. K. opened the door. She led us through a hallway. There was a big cat sitting in the middle of her kitchen, a gray and black striped tabby with a wonderfully white chest.

"That's not Cleo," said Seymour. "Not by a long shot."

"That's Sid," said Ms. K. "He belongs to me, and this morning he snuck out when I went for the paper. He knows he's not supposed to. He wasn't very sorry when he returned either. I believe he made a new acquaintance."

She moved the kitchen curtain aside. We looked out. Sitting on the back fence, cleaning her soft calico coat and looking very pleased with herself, was the most beautiful cat in the world.

And that's why, when Gran came back from Hawaii, all four of her cats were safely at home to greet her.

Kink. Max. Killer. And Cleo.

Chapter 15

Of course that isn't the end of the story. I should have guessed what happened next, but I didn't. I didn't know then that stories about cats don't ever end.

Life went back to normal for a while. Actually it was better than normal. Our hardware store now carries pet supplies. I am in charge of them. Fridays after school and Saturday afternoons I choose what to order, count what comes in and stock the shelves. Seymour helps out when he can. And the rest of the week, even though I miss Mom and Dad because they are at the store so much, at least I know they miss me too.

About two months later Gran invited Seymour and me to her house.

Max was there. He was sitting in a flowerpot.

Kink was there. He was playing with a dancing spot of sunlight on the wall.

Killer was there. She was watching us from beneath the heavy fronds of a fern.

Cleo was there. She was nestled in a beautiful basket with two new kittens.

"Kittens!" said Seymour. "Cleo's got kittens!"

"When did it happen?" I asked.

"I read lots about kittens," said Seymour. "Their eyes are open so they must be a week old at least."

"Just a little more than a week," said Gran. "I'm sorry I didn't tell you right away, but I wanted to give Cleo a chance to learn to be a good mother before she had visitors."

"They're so little!" I said.

They were two little fluff balls. One was striped black and gray with two white front mittens. The other was calico

— not the muted colors of gray and salmon like Cleo, but bright orange, pure black and lots of white. Cleo looked very proud of them.

"That's why she ran away!" I said.

"When a female cat wants to find a father for a batch of kittens, there isn't much that can be done to stop her," said Gran. She reached down to pat Cleo. "But these will be her only kittens. This time we really are going to visit the vet."

"Good plan," said Seymour. "In five years, two cats can turn into sixty-five thousand cats."

"Sixty-five thousand. Are you sure, Seymour?" asked Gran.

"I didn't check the math myself," said Seymour, "but that's what the books said."

"My goodness," said Gran.

Killer walked over and sat protectively by the kitten basket. Cleo began to lick the kittens.

"Speaking of big numbers," said Gran. "Six cats are going to make quite a house-full around here. I was wondering,

I was hoping, I wanted to ask ..."

I looked at Gran. She didn't usually beat around the bush.

"TJ, I know you didn't really like cats when you agreed to cat-sit for me," said Gran.

"You knew?" I asked. "You knew all along?"

"I knew," said Gran. "But you always treat animals kindly, which is why I could ask you. And you had time to spend with them. That's important. And I was wondering if somewhere along the line you might have, that is, maybe they kind of ..."

Gran took a deep breath.

"TJ, would you be interested in cat-sitting these kittens when they get a little older — permanently?"

Cat-sit the kittens? Permanently! Even when they're cats!

"I don't know," I said. "Mom and Dad ..."

"I've talked to them," said Gran. "They said they don't dislike cats as much as they used to. They'll let you have the kittens if that's what you'd really like."

Was that what I'd really like?

"You could call the striped one T-Rex," said Seymour. "T-Rex with little white mittens."

"And I could name this one ..." I began. "I could name this one ..."

It was crazy, but I didn't feel I had a right to take them unless I could think of a name. It was a test. Seymour had already passed it. Even though he couldn't have the cats at his house, he'd thought of a really neat name.

But I couldn't think of one. My mind was blank. I had to think of something!

Suddenly I remembered the phone bill. It had arrived a few weeks ago and my mom had almost fainted.

"Alaska," I said.

Even as I said it, the name seemed to fit. There was a lot of white on this littlest of kittens — I was pretty sure there was a lot of white snow in Alaska. And the name had an adventurous ring to it.

"I could name this one Alaska," I said. "And I'd love to take them both."

It's hard to say no to the world's

greatest grandmother — but that's not why I adopted the kittens.

I adopted T-Rex and Alaska because maybe, just maybe, I like cats after all.

The following books provided the facts for:

THE AMAZING CAT REPORT
by TJ and Seymour

(They received a mark of 10 out of 10 — the exact same mark as Amanda.)

Eric Allan and Lynda Bonning, *Everycat*, Allen & Unwin, Australia, 1985

Lynn Allison, *How To Talk To Your Cat*, Globe Communications, New York, 1993

Gladys Baker Bons, *Album of Cats*, Rand McNally, New York, 1971

Roger A. Caras, *A Cat is Watching*, Simon and Schuster, New York, 1989

Bruce Fogle, *101 Questions Your Cat Would Ask Its Vet*, Carroll & Graf Publishers, New York, 1993

Gail Gibbons, *Cats*, Holiday House, New York, 1996

Barbara Shook Hazen, *The Dell Encyclopedia of Cats*, Delacort Press, New York, 1974

Barbara Hehner, *Let's Find Out About Cats*, Random House, Toronto, 1990

Michael Homan, *Cats*, Franklin Watts, London, 1976

Fernand Mery, *The Life, History and Magic of The Cat*, Grosset and Dunlap, New York, 1968

Desmond Morris, *Catlore*, Jonathan Cape, London, 1987

Desmond Morris, *Catwatching*, Jonathan Cape, London, 1986

Alice Philomena Rutherford, *The Reader's Digest Illustrated Book of Cats*, Reader's Digest Association (Canada), Montreal, 1992

Millicent E. Selsam, *How Kittens Grow*, Four Winds Press, New York, 1973

David Taylor, *The Ultimate Cat Book*, Simon and Schuster, New York, 1989

Michael Wright and Sally Walters, *The Book of The Cat*, Pan Books, London, 1980

photo: Ted Hutchins

Hazel Hutchins is one of those rare writers whose stories breathe laughter and tears together. Her characters are real, their predicaments funny and tough. She is the author of many beloved books for children, including chapter books *Within a Painted Past* and *The Three and Many Wishes of Jason Reid*, and picture books *One Dark Night* and *Tess*. *TJ and the Cats* is her first book with Orca Book Publishers. Hazel lives in Canmore, Alberta, with her husband and her cats.

105